The Logic of the Stairwell

The Logic of the Stairwell
and Other Images

Marc Atkins

Shearsman Books
Exeter

First published in the United Kingdom in 2011 by
Shearsman Books
58 Velwell Road
Exeter EX4 4LD

http://www.shearsman.com/

ISBN 978-1-84861-161-0

Acknowledgements

Rod. Michel. Françoise. Eve.

Contents

The Logic of the stairwell   7

Places Found and Imagined   25

The Damned   37

The Journey to an Empty Room   43

Awake in a Room   49

Shorts   61

Synopses   69

THE LOGIC OF THE STAIRWELL

Fifty thousand greying silhouettes at the Falls of Terni found refuge in the dying heat of a damp Autumn afternoon. Friedrich hid none too well the many shadows across his eyes as he spoke in lucid tone of the inequalities of the surfaces and how long a serious discussion should be held on the popularity of playing underwater with tubercular mothers. It was something under a decade ago that due to the loss of insufficient childless couples in the streets of Paris I found myself in an unenviable position alongside the possessor of three of the most sought after images by the long missed short deceased inventor Professor P. Emanuel P. Reuse. Pictures further that could only be seen by way of the 'lamp that stands in a corner' a curious invention consisting of one standard standard lamp and a corner.

Through grounds of tender delights and desolate eyes we paced alongside these placed days seeing little observing much. While fifty thousand silhouettes in attendance at the burial of Leo Tolstoy in the unprepossessing and yielding year of my dear grandfathers birth 1910 stood bent with decapitated heads and a little gristle showing. There was indeed something of a way to go.

Walking the fields that very day picking at left behind picnic scabs from carpet burn Virginia Sackville-West 168 searches once more for her lost sister a ritual only the father could fathom though being somewhat missing presumed incoherent somewhere in the high mountains near Albi he could offer no sound explanation. Absent at birth Virginia distrusted her dark hair and pail green framed mirror. In a fine evening light the two younger siblings planted a field of flowers selectively bleaching them to spell out "anon" since when each day as if cursed ordered curious or surprised Virginia would cross under the motorway interchange and trace a balanced way down to the lake to look again for the place her great aunt had mentioned in a last note to an unborn child.

Black trees cut from the backdrop of a motorway sunrise incline towards ideas for music where tintinnabulation resonates from collective strain. I dream of reading like watching the fine scratches of rain drop and tear a little at the fabric of thought. Awake I am a stranger in my own mind an ausländer naked in the snow a foreigner in an alien landscape who does not speak his own language.

Baleful and transient the wind blew the telephone wires attached to their taut poles out across the desert. Pleading voices lay pleading while recipients lay relieved. Verticality uprightness and linear perspective dismissed with a 'pah'.

What are these cities seen from the corner of the eye standing and withering with no recognition or the chance to tell epiphytic stories. There is always someone who knows nothing. There she walked dust in her hair dressed like liquid light a sentient being whose nurse broke all her promises saying this was that and all social fall out was the price to be paid for being good. A mouth like wisdom on Wednesday amid steps that don't heal her name is in her head dead head. What spurts from the spine is not nor was ever fluid but compacted eventuality a shrieking face without freedom quietly and unassailably voiced.

– Oh dear

– Oh dear what?

– My head hurts

– Oh dear

– Oh dear what?

– Your head hurts.

Juliet Margaret ran the risk of falling into place. Her black stockings worn through from walking the roof tiles at dawn hair asunder flesh a dripping marrow. The breakfasts were high and pleasant however though with little room for discussions on time honoured subjects. Pour yourself another lesson. The view from a low brick perhaps.

Watch the lights come on. Offer an easy aside. See being seen not keep secrets. Suppress your fingertips grant yourself this interminable ride blunder with me eat the sensible and flood the what world you can find with mouths full of triumph. Multitude multitude a great name for a great art. Trinkets for the rich. Studies for artists. Whine as any other feeble gesture reflects well in this market with more interest than a b er. Fur lined with fine spun human fur he blanks the screen because he is not in it poor sap. Not a flesh eating internal sort but certainly at one with the pads off. His motivation being not simply illogically illegal but en rapport. Poor Eleanor May a twinkle tip violent and vision poised in blue light. Place it carefully on the window sill I'll touch it later. Cut the sash and open the fair as a hundred fine ladies hide under a box.

So down the centre lane we wandered wary of the course of carders behind each wall and musing upon the felicity of each bungled abortion. Consider that the perimeter fence subsists no bigger than your presumption. Now on you come. Words should only be heard. Just one could charm the prayers from an ebullient stick insect. These endomorphs don't gonna dance without their post-mortem picture. So equipped they take for a ride the car down by the lake where stories of shores straddle sundry islands leaving hours left to pretend they are about the city. Avoid people. Wear away the sea. Watch the sand. We are lost us both. The sky line is a burden. Lethargy collides into insights. Rare and lovely things retain the membrane of tuppenny rides. Show me a path I am pointing at yours. Step along it. Do. We should now and then administer something that has made this ageing worthwhile. Don't walk on your hands the ground is too rough. You will need to muster some enthusiasm for climbing the white they are still white aren't they stairs. Better. Next let's pretend that what we are is what we are.

Hide in a corner and watch the absurd still mirrors morph. Note the umbrae I spoke of below the liquid looking into eyes looking into eyes. Are we not becoming what we want along this fine wide wet road.

Dye your hair and all will be well. Genocide of intuition. Fifteen men lost through excessive tedium. Peripatetic jam jar sales men fight battles over forgotten children. Headlines sell faces to faces. Filter them whose lives are roped secure against excess weatherproofing. Light happens to other people. Dark swellings find their place amongst the foreign chatter where misspellings are something to live with like lung decease sic. Let me find a route to the preserved plasmic hearts of things for the reckoning of the dead and force quit dog's bark leaves only a sad demise for the early to bed. What a lark. Up in splendour take your vows slap the roof pay for what is yours fluid beetle lemon and a dash of acrid spittle does so make the womb ache. The enlightening horror of a sitting devil lifting his hat being a happy childhood memory. An image that testifies to a great mind but for them. No problem here wall me in raising vapour the torture chamber is where veracity states that polythene wrapped thoughts create patterns where there was once a just and calm flatness. I am again on the forgotten path dreaming of hanged chandeliers and typographic errors. Quickly furnish me with your books so I can no longer walk as there soon will be no need to. Elaine Talbot woke feeling unlucky. Nearly the first to the floor the latter day sports teacher came first. Grouts with everything. Ginger taste spoils all sees the blithe leading the blithe pigs cage doors open sore to the touch feel compassion for the noises outside or was it inside I forget now. Still I fear for us. The weight of the fate of the day is spiralling treacle. Wherever we go our saliva can be diluted only by the water of another planet. The rats have a language of their own fooling all but you and your. Blemished smiles fall so far in the past indoor rivers flavour and savour the desperate memories' memories. If a photograph could be of shadow instead of its replacement. Base thoughts. Sow to speak. Appropriate faux cards. May be when the chicken is unstuffed and don't the sprouts taste better after falling on the floor. Quickening the pace. And so Mr. Blight ate with her fingers today.

Today I remember I looked out across a great plane and saw two umbrous figures walking towards me. Divided they walked passed and disappeared into my shadow. Don't change subjects. Who governs who in this languid land beyond our nearest telephone operator. Flat sky flat earth. Like the bomb didn't drop. How to guess the length of the collective shadow. Light is time. Shade is space. Kazimir Malevich saw fifty thousand days and fifty thousand hours add up to a blackening square.

Story telling is blurred edges. Worn points fit snugly like wet beds. I hear voices through a wall. File down the crowd and pepper the roads. You should walk in front as I have bombs to watch for. Blanket cover the dry earth so the damp will stay in our heads and incoherent insects will no longer be troubled by flapping thoughts.

Trudge.

And so found we arrived at the edge of the city dark from the burned forest bruised from a fill of bad literature. An unsure house it was that presented itself and before a pause we regarded ourselves barely perceptibly enter it. There we long dwelt our search continuing through crystallised shadows for the nature of our journey. Nights seemed to again pass unheard. And the dust fell. Through an eternity of rooms a drifting heat haze shimmered in vapoury light save that there was no warmth nor feint of dawn. Standing in a pause we watched. We found shadows in the darkness as darkness is the cast of shadows. Smouldering in redolence the house suffered our presence *coup de foudre*. Hanging in a pause we watched. We were imbedded here. A story in form. Content through existence. An exercise in meaning gives that thought never disappears only misplaces to a place where all that has been forgotten finds its way.

Better to sleep no sleep than dream no dream. Illustrate in soft white chalk the time line of a caress now try to gently open the cupboard door to see your shilling still rolling in the dust. I chose a street. Your turn to find another light source. A cave is where a hundred thousand rosaries hang upside down though not to upset the cleaner who does all the picking up. *The Lacemaker* is over there on the stairs in naked sufferance as she is the only one able to work in chronological thirds. See the absence of light against the riser. Thirst for brutality where that gentler hand is or was a conquest for banality. Agree then post me another image of the Michelangelo *David* I've forgotten the colour of its eyes. The Uffizi will never flood again I've seen to it. I took a photograph and told the world that is how it is supposed to be. Now then.

For a while we sat and whiled away watching the doings and comings pass us by.

Straying further into the focus of our meandering route de terre each bridge cooling our unfanned flesh each door openly smiling an unfathomable volley of foreign blanks our uneven binary steps predicted the events to come. Well it is a plan as far as muzzy theories go.

The tunnel interlarded with intrepid gems lead us down into a place not quite resembling the night. The film was now running dry. As the mercury vaporised the danger became that there would be no one left to believe us. Making images by making images is surely enough in a historyless world. On we foraged by the now and then flash of a dysfunctional light beaming at what there was to beam at. Sound the horn should any ridiculous type want to follow us. It's no use claiming we are not from round here these foreigners don't play a straight leg being keen to back flap then lay claim to their country. Further offended they are when offering you their shirt you tell them to stop blowing bubbles at their admirals. Best left grinning at each other.

Suppurating alliances. In a cool world the lips of the lost suck in protracted thoughts while clouding their ears against the gravel of wailing *putti*. Nonplussed we bake in the hot sun lounging to the brevity of our mistakes our regrets and the lifting of frigid sweaters.

Tranquillity.

Behold another dark pool. Who hasn't one nowadays. But still murk's aside a choice spot this look see the mountains from here do for the snows' high capped the flowerless garden grand and all the people who walk therein posed.

aim came dame fame game lame maim name same tame

Night rippled through me in naked rhythms. We

sat around our meagre fire with eager appetites pulling the strings that made angels drop from the sky. Go treat yourself to a wing and the whalebone corset soup. The dark is lightening against our backs as night draws off and dawn pours from the hot tap unbosoming yet again a scummy sky. Standing deranged we begin once more as Dr. Welshborne our sometime companion an infant among men lollops off in any direction pleased to deal in false memories being a fellow not at all happy to deal with his own.

Potted *poésie* is a stinking mess of burning money. Frightened women bear witness to the demoralised men tearing at the walls. There for all to see. Laughing behind a rash of small windows. Could be a punishment to the poor. Lick the weeping bowl syphoning from the elegant sore we must away to polish off our delusions.

The journey continued into an asymmetric land glazed and jocund. It was in a room under the upstair where we found the floors met the walls and while stumbling over the many cracks we each discovered something left in a corner. But slowly it dawned that with nothing to leave in its place we had now become encumbered by responsibility. So. Take it or the memory. A bell rang and tapping wandered down the treads. We groaned in sleep complaining of the other that the other was inconsiderate lying so close to the dead. Here where we are nothing but what we create these shadowed hours I see now are the only place to live. None can see us and we see none. Everything is thought so all is invention. QED. Having stared into the morning we trace

17

its backlit prop onto the backdrop. Come let's take what we have and rewrite what we have never done.

Sleep is a plastic wrapped suffocation chamber. It is the room which enters you pouring acrid light over healing thoughts and exposes them with razor scaled endoscopes. Sleep is a damp collection of some tedious answers.

Look how skinny you have become. There just there no just there steady ahh damn missed it again that fleet footed thought which never quite comes into focus. Could that it would answer every riddle and put all anxieties at ease. We pilgrimaged to the perimeter fence as there is always something without. We found expectation easing its grip. There are many good things in my pantry but none of which I want whereas you my lopsided friend know truly what you want and what you want is to stand in a quiet room. I will see again the blank skies reflected in her blank eyes staring at the hole that falls through the earth where the tumour was removed with despicable sorrow. Each tower and mountain is focused cogitation where each street and valley is putrefying flesh. Forgiven tongues don't answer. Foreign tongues lick the sweat from your neck. Forgotten tongues plead silently and never let you go.

Our brains are wrapped in cellophane. The city looks better with the curtains closed. The tap dripping reminds us that you are the long dead.

For a thousand years we have held this pinnacle and watched the cavernous world sweep down away before us. But as all dreams come in the dying seconds of sleep our journey together has taken but a moment of time. I hear monochrome voices deliver instructions to the sound of a slow metronome.

Fall.

Wait one more moment. In the scent of caverns where no light spoils the view I see the great expanse of flat desert stretch out towards the distant haze. She stands with mud on her hands her silent flesh unmoved by this screaming air. Undulating movies flickered against the dripping wall and in-depth commentators comment quietly on the scene. Serenity looms over blood splattered cave paintings and makes her mark. Scurrying feet shout and bawl lapping up each plate in turn. Through wintery darkness the child drinks supplicating water which between sips flows down hill and away to the far concrete planes. So there are the stairs dark amongst the shadows rippling scarce defining a story of ascent documenting decent. Well it is either there or not do not deny seeing the lighthouse but see its light. Walking beside me you still do not know my name. I wake with the fall of dust each morning its binary nitrates dripping onto my pale skin yet all there is to show for it are these broken ropes. No pity.

We once spoke together of the logic of the stairwell.

Afterwords

I

Sip the day. Entering a long room long lost images slip by before me. We rode on at a loss and promise keeping a pace in step for a bed was at every mile. Should you pull me gently into your loving corner set adrift those careless enough to be walled in. I am the dawn and the dusk pity that when caressing my deadly lungs. Watch for the famous patients who hide an array of tortured calotypes in their flower baskets. Those poor curbmen jostle with ample hearts but with skewers drawn they will offer patents on every hole dug. With unhelpful fidelity each coroner present a selection of gelatine pictograms which follow in logical sequence. Fourteen foot tapeworms may be a blind but what wonderful decorations they make. It's tiring here with grumbling eyes heavy stomach and a pen and ink that has better ideas. Look at those down there in a dead heap and when too tired drizzle on the light. It feels good keeping faith in these greying days when the tired mind returns to some vague memory of home.

II

Palatine's gentle undulations carry me far. Stare at the door until it unlocks. Fellow humans write a note to plait formed spirits speeding by on wearily mounted trains. Trumpets horn the carnage arrives news papers begrudgingly wave as tired souls turn a page. Feed me on unsurity for all I need lies there in. Pulling at sores bleeds. All roads appeared at once as the beckoning minstrels were sent to count our marks. What fools we are the trumpets sound and when the final trains roll on we should put aside each word as one. But empty headed we all fall down. The sun leaks blood on teaselled down. Pull us from our body bags power lines scratches through seamless dreams. Finally almost all we need is almost all there is it seems.

III

Draw a line in the water press the figures dots will do for eyes the backs are turned any way as we hovered behind the mountain watching the lone man salute the mist alone should one day he discover us and one of his or her meritorious glorious dead read the lengthened silver that passes for shadow behind us for we too suffer the fate of hate of those living in windless marks as grain not quite ground sand blocked by green palter was named.

IV

Active. Empty.

Places Found and Imagined

The lights in slo-mo pass and the soft moss weeps under a leaden dawn. With cracking breaths the straggling I lies down to sleep in melismatic drift. The moon backs behind mottled glass and the western mountains agonise beneath damp skies. I dreamt in sketchy rhymes of the road that basks in a rain storm. Heavy eyes carry across the sweep of land while footing the hills the village ensconced presents itself in flapping shutters and wounded walls. Small homes sitting grit-like in a sponge. As immutable crimes play out on the dull green shores villagers with peanut shell faces think of each other as a misplaced past. Where children feign dying on the fireside rugs the shrill brethren in a peeling temple look out across their de-saturated Elysium. Strung up roadkill on the hunter's fence bleeds on the passers by as they hungrily pay for terminal rations. The poor boy weeping to punish his subdued friend finally bolts for the door. Fornicators crawl home pausing now and then at the sounds of the spitting light. A guilty step in the thick layer of angel dust soot like plumes a little.

Fade to dark.

The blackness grays then blues. Lento the humming hours slide past in unmeasureable tones. The quiet casts across the fading picture that hangs on the white wall. I sit back to the warmth of an autumn fire and watch through the ashen windows the small turbulences of a minor day. From the distant hills no wind bends the abject tree. An unaccompanied crow arcs slow-winged through the mist. Dogs *sotto voce* bark on the thin air. The monumental clouds expeditiously reform. Events calm. At the last temper of evening the fulvous light flares at the tips of things. And this distant room dies.

Fade to dark.

Sleep on. Keep looking.

Where you stand stay quiet. Grasp a small breath. Watch the alien light crackle and fragment. The city is emptying before you. Step from the water and leave behind a wake. Climb steadily across your discordant thoughts. Feed on the effigies of your abased ancestors. In the semi-shade a sleeping rook looks into a disconcerted eye. You are now where the rainwater washes war mud from the abandoned pavements. Reid your feit. Reed your feint. Read your fate. Consider the air on such a morning. Quiet. Damp. Grey. Here in this room the silence cannot be broken. Of leaving. Find a way on this tragic day. You turn and answer the cries from the empty square. Through the distorted glass again I see you. I stay the flow of light around your insoluble eyes peel the fluid from your ungated mouth and drive away the doubt about your deft ears.

At the end of the pier she stands watching the dawn light spark against the water. The early breeze abrades her hair with her blue dress. Translucent flesh absorbs the freshly damp air. From a distant room the mother's voice carries past. The light curtain hanging in the winter sun rustles at the warmth of the heater perched on the wooden box. Grey eyes watching small things.

In the air of October from this place of rapturous

visions I look out past the tepid window through the chill mist at the damp rocks the windblown leaves and the cloud-wrapped hills towards the distant place that claims to calm the uneasy mind. The sunlight casts through the open door where the naked woman in the ancient kitchen washes herself at the stand of a blue-flowered bowl. Spilled water soaks with ease into the stone tiles.

To a coast of eyes we abandon ourselves.

As it is I am here lit soft by the indifferent reflection of a flaking mirror. As it is on this dread day the light moves only to obscure. Something waits there beyond where time stops. Attentive. Reflecting.

In the silent world of hell the birds sing. Though somewhere distant. Far off. The mist lies across vast fields where the humid air of an entombed morning bruises the skin. Look levelly out at the landscape and see as an émigré the stillness. Remember the occupied lives never to return. The orange lights on the remote hills reflect as a body against the night clouds. Taken up. Like a spaceship.

The rain blows in through the half open window dampening the single bed of torn sheets. A buzzing off-station TV furnishes the only light in the room. From the street we watch through the window the three coruscate lit forms. The heavy rain fractures the lights of the street lamps and dances writhing shadows against the deformed glass. It pours into our face as we looked up to see the three silhouettes flickering against the glass. In wet bodies we watch. Our eyes for a while wander off across neighbouring buildings looking from window to window. We wonder at the contents of these satellite worlds. Screened-off biographies. Implodes in a vacuum. The building has a rail bridge cutting across the street into its form dissecting the rooms. Architecture to hide people. We draw back to the window. Watching the shadows with intent. Not seeing them. Inside looking out or outside looking in. The journey as the rain had never stopped.

In the wake of indefinite verse this icy tongue bleeds with broken words dripping from its insidious mouth. When eating nettles from the dark plate the shrill tones of your other voice queries your thoughts in silence. We call on a single deed from all those who stand present. Listen to our meaning. Redefine the states of unease. Make plain the plan to abandon the cage.

Each one falls unseen into the stone cast waters.

My mind is emptying. To think is to fear. Letters in a book are patterns drawn in ink. I am dogged by the thoughts of a lost man. Standing in the street I failed to notice the pity of a reluctant recluse. I saw him once on the top-deck of a bus. I photographed him with his name a halo upon his head.

Send me to the place you call land. Show me the lanes that wind through the dwellings of your aphonic belief. For all the many towers will one day fall from the skyline. Hesitate at the occasional word. Find me out amongst the settling seeds as they drag me underground to await transmutation. With torch or lamp I still cast a shadow. Beside the wall.

Walking one step beside another reminds me of you. Pour the wine. Wait in line. As you see. Forerunners of the past. We wait in line. Feel along a little more and you will touch the last house on the beach before the sheer cliff. Fall or just linger the juncture. Don't care. I will stand over there. They understand this is only a rehearsal. See them all slide without effort around the street corners. It helps that the tide is coming in. With something new to look at each one abjures the wait. Only when the shining stones are out of reach. Say nothing.

Find the meaning in the title. The rest is explanation.

How sordid is a soul. Nothing more than a traumatic heart bleeding an uncorroborated testimony. There they lie. A world of contaminated finger nails scratching into flesh. Enduring the daily dive through the layers of others' stories. Relive the hours that bind you to your past. There in the pretty little box found to keep them fast in. But don't tell. Stand beside me for a while and watch for the stranger. Don't swivel your head. Face forward and move only your eyes. The hours pass. You stand transfixed by the stillness. All moves before you. Hold tight. It is life that grows here about. There will be a day when it is all you will want. A low-tone quiet murmurs about this place. Don't you think. There is a big machine somewhere clocking you in. Be quicker. You don't want to be paying for more hours than you have. I wouldn't want that. All day sweeping primordial life back into the sea. The things people thought of. To stop yet more gods coming in. Just nail the lacemaker's skirt to a big rock. Still.

The sun's out now. Let's play on that bench over there. All the flesh you can slice. Apply a little pressure here. Purloin more of the fruit from that anthropic salesman. Off to bite more smiles from a threadbare town.

Fly silently across a scumbling sky.

Tired of looking at myself reflected in these ageing glass pains. I am no more than a projection against the night. The great fire burns behind the silhouetted trees. They stand and die beyond the jealous glass. With the warmth at my back the cast of morning filters through the condensation that has gathered to the corners of the small glass. So the wind blows and my days dissolve. A listing vessel wandering out onto the great plane. The breeze whipping the long grass around a hollow form and billowing off into an incomprehensible rift. Understand me now. Feel the sodden wood beneath my feet. Gather your thoughts like the scattering leaves. We can only slip and fall between the cracks of our own image.

She sits in the watchtower arrow at the ready. Her petrified arms sicken for a stroke. Polluted eyes fading out. The colourless landscape is the unmissable target. The friction-less trees are toppling row by row. In the fire above the steam a phantom of hunters pass their way home. A murmuring song.

Once unlocked from the cellar the monochrome kite bears us far from the castle. We walked the predawn path past the real trees once thought backdrops and disappear beyond the rise. A promising darkness gently envelops us as there on a safe rock we will one day sit crying. And when the shallow tide comes in we will watch the atramental plane fly over and on toward the distant black hills.

Well the sun rose and woke the myriad piceous butterflies who hid from us the fields in which we could rest. So laying on a heathen mound till noon we slept. The air thick. We were shadows in small places. Our dreams a papier-mâché vale.

Thoughts like flakes of sweat. A florescent mask and a pale breast. Dancing flat against the wall the leaden cracks stink of blood. I'm falling in a blackened hole. Witness to a dark world. A sinking shrinking gagging space. A fragmenting tower. A rotting crop.

With lucid barks at moon washed dusts that float and fall in eddying grains we pull the words from frothing mouths the ones they wrote with ulcer'd tongues. Our minds stop working at three a.m. We broke a step that filled our path. We slunk into the looted mall where all the world had come to laugh. We pulled up short at the feeding zeal that echoed round the absurd isles and found a gang of fighting moms awash with sell by rancid waste. The finest that the beast can sell the best of everything we need a little prod at infant guilt and credit absolution's taste. The fitted man stands tall to tell the secret of our reborn youth to grab all that is here and now and disdaining antecedent truth.

The night is lifting the lid of this winter sky. I listen. The old lampshade gunmetal sent ringing against the porch wall by the evening sail. Occasional snow falling around my slippered feet I stand remembering as a child a first realisation of the sweet air of a winter dusk. Thoughts uttered without resonance crash my mind. Thoughts spilling like intestines from a sliced gut. I fear even these concrete clouds. Nothing happened to me. My life is a story I once heard. This very present I can hardly grasp therefore all else must be hearsay. I ran along the shoreline of dreams. The waiting moon spat at the sea. Twisted illusions entangled my next step. Infected lungs gasped for clean air. On I ran.

Fade to black.

Are you in there. Do you too stand at a window peering into an ice-wind darkness through nebulous breaths. The light is impenetrable. Your reflection beckons me out into the night. Your fingertips touch mine through the glass as if though the ice-sheet of a frozen lake. To melt the ice-bound water would be to liquify time. I long to swim down into the past and touch your warm fingers once more. But now we are lost in the dark. Our reflected revenants no more than memories apparent.

It was barely night as I pulled off highway 80 into the gas station. The dull pierce of unwashed red neon and green fluorescent swam about my stripped eyes. After the sundry miles of darkening landscape and one point perspective it was like passing thought the iridescence of a bubble's skin. Far off to the right I could see the fireflies of a city pinpricked from the dark plain.

Sinking finally into the rotting tree which stands before the long avenue leading to the end of this vast night the wind gasped amongst the branches and the flesh that grew

34

from the cracks in the bark. I pull back the folds and leak from the putrid history into a sage air which clings to me as a bewildering love about my neck. Then turning into a distant past the world becomes dissolute. An unbending alternative. A way out of the inevitable fortune of another vision. Panning through the distraught hours I stick in the corrosive mud and wait for your now tepid touch to drag me desolate from acedia. A breath on me. I await the coming of the sapphire wings that bathe quietly on a warm road and to finish my interminable history. In your head the poison could never pardon the pain. Bleed on the hand which carries your image. I think of myself crushing your heart in the reflection of an eye. I tell a story where my eyes are bound my ears shrouded and my mouth arid. Then follow this ineffectual body into the storms that sweep over the places of other lives. It was then you answered all my questions. The house. Then the empty rooms. Who held the insoluble you.

And our tears fall away into the silence.

The tenebrae invite us in. So perched we upon the lifeless bow wilt and slip into the brine. A pubescent soul. A taciturn act. Reminding us of our grieving days when necessarily we left before the final blow. Yowl. You are as you are. I am equal in size to all things.

You pressed the buttons in the right order. 07 Le Cri. In the triangle of acid sun light catches the corner of the window frame set in the attic roof. You lie secretly in the shade of your lair looking up at the heaven's blue and white underbelly sliding past the square fissure. What cares as the great stones fall to earth.

Where the moon slides over charged ice naked feet crack across rimy earth and eyes cast over a petrified land. And there we remain outside the gates. Of the land beyond the wasted city. In a curious play a hypaethral cranium positioned on the table between us tilts slightly.

The morning sun slides down the window pooling on the sill.

I watch the unhurried rain fall.

In a tenuous hand I move to make notes on places found and imagined.

Hard teeth bite into the detested liquid. Each drop etching the heart. We have seen neither walls nor doors today. And from the hearth the lines blown torn and darkened have become meaningful words. Hold the seance a little longer. Time has seeped from the room. Neither clock nor mirror retains memories. A fine rain of thoughts has become a mist.

I sat afloat the glassy lake. Beyond the window the world slowed. Becoming hardly visible. Hardly audible. Of neither taste or tangibility. Timeless still. The rain undressed the morning. The shadows shallowed. Colours scarcely a bleached reflection. I turned off the lamp and sat beside the window in the pool of subdued light that without effort drained into the room.

THE DAMNED

The days began spreading like wildfire.

The train burns into the night. Floating amongst the dark the orange stations are unattainable escape routes holding still as I turn and catch them scream past.

Five weeks hiding in rooms I never found. A vacant place with a thin mattress. Photographs letters and notebooks lying in unstacked piles on the floor. A humming silence muffled the air. Ripped wallpaper and worn carpets stained. Three floor-to-ceiling windows overlooked a two-lane highroad. The frequent noise of traffic sustained me through lonely hours. Confused by mental nausea and the uncertainty of the images I lay making stories from the patterns on the ceiling. Between times I searched the windows on the opposite side of the wide street following the systems of lives beyond each of the glass borderlines. Nights of violent orange blue and volatile red green leapt out and clung to the dark. In the daylight hollow rooms were still shadows. Dull matted shrouds twitched in a broken breeze. Shades buried themselves deep within the futile space. Uncommonly a face appeared. A mist of breath on the glass. Staring at the cold. Looking. Like mine.

They lay amongst the razed buildings and rough grass stars glinted through the glowing air that carried above the city. The animate lights of the approximate motorway reflected keenly in the sisters' eyes. The camera beside them lay burdened. Through the dark a boy walks in the dampened air. From the glare of the carriageway lamps he discerned the figures lying on moulds of debris. At the sound of stumbling footsteps the three rose and strained stares into the darkness. There was the noise of the traffic and there was silence. The youngest sister picked up the camera and pointed it towards the glancing perturbation. Pressing the shutter the flash fired. Revealed in the instant of light the naked boy froze against the purple night sky. The moment then passed in the dark. Scrambling hands and feet scraped over rubble faintly cutting through the sounds of the tearing traffic.

I woke behind the storm of black hair. Enveloping her taught flesh and paralysing scent I did not know I was screaming. There in that place. Not going where I wanted to go.

You are where I cannot find you.

Do not go.

We stand within the threshold of rooms.

Haunted.

She sat in the shadow of the back room watching through the door the men walk the far room. Pacing the floor the heavy sunlight through the blinds rendered each a slatted silhouette.

I saw the two photographs a year ago. Set upright on a mantelpiece leaning against an enamelled cigarette box alongside several others. The first a blurred image of a woman bleached hair standing with a camera over her shoulder. The backdrop a city at dusk. The second a man's face half shadowed. So close you could see the pores of his skin and the dimples on the red stained linoleum behind his head. The wound across his cheek and the flow of blood to the floor was inexorable.

The door gave with a gentle crack. I pushed it open and walked into a dim room. A few steps disturbing the flawless dust made my eyes water. I saw the two coats hanging on brass pegs screwed to the back of the bedroom door. I found the small photograph in the lower inside left pocket of the dark grey coat. Not where she said it would be.

I crawled over to the stiff upright chair snatching at shallow breaths. Pulling myself up I sat back into it. The image of a woman I once saw through a railway carriage window brushing her black hair fired across my eyes.

Sitting on the bed I caught her reflection glance the hallway mirror. That was the last time I saw M. As the years pass that final brief image has stayed vivid in my mind where all other memories of her have bleached out.

He stood on the empty road looking up at the windows. To his left the sun was setting behind the vast ironwork of skeletal skyscrapers. To his right an encroaching purple sky pushed cool air along the street. He ran his eyes along the tower of glass. There was the forth floor and there the third window from the right. An unhealthy shadow passed out through the glass. He took paper and pen from his pocket and made brief an observation. Returning the pen and paper to pocket he turned head down and walked west.

Yet on the brightest of days the air under the Viaduct is dim. This drizzle on a winters afternoon. This shelter. This place deep like an atavistic cave. I waited. The soluble light changed. The temperament of the street shifted. The dust began to fall.

Memories of the empty room echo through my head. I taste the lemon on my breath as the chill begins to lift. The sun's morning rays spill over the roofs on the other side of the river. I haven't eaten for days. Where is she. Thoughts of her used to be intermittent. I suspect she will bring the letter. I watch her walk across the water towards me.

Journeying troubles the mind. Between the place where I am and the place I will be is arid land.

Idly I pored though the note books and photographs which were strewn across the floor. The earliest I marked dated back some twenty years. In time I understood each as simply a suicide note.

I will remember you as the last grains fall through the hourglass.

The Journey to an Empty Room

At night the desert is water beneath my feet.

I journeyed to an empty room. A place waiting. A drowning chamber.

The desert is a life calm and barren to the starry eye. In the stillness of freezing thought I dissolve like burning plastic into the sand. Across the plane unattainable the cold horizon shimmers.

In the limbo room the door to the left is always ajar. To the right the window is closed and nail locked. The blood stained plank attached to the wall beside the door frame out of which a long spike sticks is no longer there. I stand in the room and watch my body melt across the deserted floor. Lifting the roof and stepping into the blue-grey city the night is warm and the monochrome sky motionless. The storm has passed. The air waits. I am alone in this watchful place scattered by the wet streets. Clouds billow from some windows. Orange lights from others. The end of the street falls away into the void. And to the void I yield.

On the daybed she sits reading from an album of photographs lost to the sound of distant music. She rarely speaks. She smiles distrait after we have kissed. She is now as she has ever been. The obligatory white face. Dark around her eyes. And her mouth the deepest red. With a thirty-something voice standing in a thirties-something dress she turns her lightly freckled face to the foxed mirror. Tears run down my face forming blue figurines. Once I knew her name. It is cold. I am her anonymity. Here before a woman whose face reflects in my eyes.

The pages of the book lying on the floor near the open window rustle. I turned my attention from the silent road of traffic far below to this small noise. The book lies quiet half shadowed by moonlight.

The life I have here in my hands is coming apart. Its scar covered form of rotting flesh and tender new buds has been falling away from me for many nights now. This thing though hardly aware I have carried all my days. Gaining weight as it fades this perfect form once shone almost floating from my hands as if eager to reach out and touch all. Its shape is a deformity. From what I can see of its insides where it was once a swirl of vivid colour it is now sluggish and pastel. I am told it is possible to unstitch this wonderful thing from my skin release it and walk away. But I can be nothing unless drawn to its demise.

I saw a head in a room. It was facing towards a table on which an open book was propped. I heard a voice describing the method of seeing as being a process where the brain produces a pulse of particular light which projects out through the eyes and onto the object being observed. Sound darkens around my ears. The air dampens and the hum of life around me becomes dull-edged. Moving through the world my looking bounces off the desperate faces of objects rather than being absorbed by them.

I slide down the wall to the warped once wet floorboards. Sitting within the brooding stillness of the dry dust I watch the undulation of shadows measure a journey across the decaying floor. I see now that these are the only hours of a life long day worth living in. These hours where unlit dreams and angelic fears drift just within reach.

With the final turning on of the dark I sit cold amongst the blackness. I feel the ineffable burden. A senseless weight burying me in mock grain. This object of nothingness clings to my skin. Tasteless it clogs my mouth. Breaths of solid air petrifying my unstretching lungs. I am frozen in its glare. It murmurs in my ears. Flecks of light spark from their friction against my eyes. Intangible fingers pick away my mind. I am in the wrong place against my will. Attacked on all sides by things that cannot move.

I lay parched of the object of light. I try to hold on to the ruptured second of twilight that fractured my fissile mind before the dark came. But even that warm blue-grey glint only echoes in the memory.

I struggle to stand. The substance of nothing presses me down. Its form as recognised and discarnate as the mirror's reflection. Unfocused patterns weave before me. Ethereal figures passing by in staccato motions. Invisible shapes groped towards. The false hope of a darker mass than the one I now endure.

I want pure light razor sharp lightness to float through for it to scratch and claw my skin draw translucent blood from each vein pale my muscles to venison flesh bleach my bones and mind to burn white to light out to purge all memory of dark.

Moths draw to me flittering against my face sensing vague memories of light. Their single desire to eat devour and smother the maddening glare.

I sit. My self a warm inferred body. An unseen unrecognised form. A vessel containing the encompassing air. Listening to the voices of an eternity of ghosts. My life is the dark. A part of its eternal state. Entire. Before all.

Infinity has seeped into me. Dissolving my body. I am atomised. Become nothing.

Awake in a Room

On a red dusty road a caught breath of heavy dawn holds me still. With thoughts in hand and sounds echoing out across early dry fields I remembered. A day when I pulled aside your hair and kissed your neck lit a fire called in sick turned off the lights and listened at the wall for the train I was sure would hit. The way I found you. Alone. A sign. On an unchanging day.

Now in the north-west corner of my room pale walls temper tepid hours revisioned words flash against pain and weeping beads of flesh sweeten an air of dubious reflection. Lying in cold breath I swelter back to that distract silence where I dream of turquoise light burning through pale dust falling across naked skin. Through an opaque roof a fevered white sky mesmerises. The walls hold steady. The floor holds steady. Memories recount only memories. Archive your dreams. Complete the slaughter in your head. End the story.

Once I would watch the city from my cellar window. The streets' myriad layered secrets called out codified in staccato rhythms. I minded your walk as your body slowly strobed past under the low lamps. Your shadow fell across my face. And never left. I hear that you stare out across a great plain. Do you see me as I lie here on this vast upper floor now so parched I hear it crack. Tell me. Am I still. Your soaked hair is battened across those fissures through which we no longer see each other. Dream me back through the miles and the years and the night rain falling hard against the windscreen of Amerigo's Russian cab. Latino. Waiting. Still.

Here small red bulbs glow in the down shade of evening. Time leaves. I step carefully down the stair to where you stand amongst the gathering crowed. In a lyrical phrase you assure the empty streets that out here no one waits. No one watches. No one forgets. When you leave you'll hide against the wall. First. Then wait. Later. When dressing in our Sunday best to protect us from the sound of falling spores breeding in the eaves as they do we may observe the yellowing shafts of light bolting downwards through the cracked roof along with the hollow sounds of the floor crumbling beneath us. However. Do look around. I believe we will find nowhere better to hide than this vacant lot. Railway engineers face the horrors of a nonparallel world and we in fine rain venture to find the distant room where answers differ as normality's lapse. Yet here we settle in an air where even the loneliest can abide. Body print your voice against the rusty wall. Talk softly when speaking to a machine. Words through blunt teeth reinstall the fallout of pain.

A slight smile echoes in the light outside. My liquid face is in the shadow part of the city. You are lost. Each step is a high heel nail. Still you breathe. Naked on the floor of this empty car park looking up at the night sky a low growl of water rises from far underground. Seeping out through the pores of the concrete it readily dampens your body trickles past your ears and winds out through the backlit streets. You wait. Staring at the stars. Breathing still.

Now I am awake. In a room. At the end of a small morning.

Again as I pull the animates to earth the ropes begin to snap. Distance grows. More permanent than some. We land on opposite coasts of a gelatine sea the cracked ends of distant lights the sibylline call to quest. On the day we left just before dawn I stood and looked across the empty runway. The silicon road that lead us here lies vitrified by the charge of a high fence. Now we are not to take our days out beyond the barricade. This theory of mind. Let me touch your abandoned breath once more. You lie in your bed a counterfeit expressionist acting out the time-lapse theatre of your mind. Cherry red runs from your mouth. Fragments of thought in dim this light grains into shade. A forced smile in a crowd of false smiles. Fear and fantasy. Stand and fall. Stand. Look. And fall.

Feverish I see skeletal trees stand black in vast yellow fields. Dulled flowers strapped to posts along country lanes wilt in memory to the distant dead. Kneeling crowds at stagnant ponds grimace at their collective reflection. Hold. Savour the last strait. Break through sieved memories. Pull the broken lockets from the nailed-to pockets and fill them with hollow looks. Throw your judgement out beyond the divide eat through the heat of the crowd press yourself against the night's pallor fight with the raging times glean each drop of dirt from her fingerprints and soften between your lips the last particle of dusk.

So I find myself without. No longer a question only fear. Love does not help against locked doors. A thousand strangers beg for hope. The woman's face cloaks in dread faith. To the oblivious man she does not exist. I dare not turn around as I see only us. As there is only us. Learn hope. Faux hope. Pretend hope. Almost hope. Careless. Remember things. Again at last. You are not here. The rail line splits and turns away into the mist. Fill the plastic buckets with bile caress the unspoilt skin and leave early to avoid the pavements and the long-handed waverers.

Via Appia. Wishing for windows where there are none the crematorium just over the forced hill crafts its walls in iced rain. Tiles unhooked slide from the roof. Further reading shows clearly the temperament on which it is built.

With blackened grins our empty nest of stainless fingers pulls us through where ganging fathers washing walls inscribe in tears of deathly waves a hissing germinal of lakes a dawn of winter's rosary in better times the blind weed bolts escapes the fields of ghosting where we bleed the coming childless haunts as solitude ingrains for each a chapter in a pageless book for blanking covers eat the verse of heavy souls still traipsing though our leaden landscapes bloody earth my sister laughing bitter dies in peace by sipping waters dry the acrid moat that floats unsought around my liquid house of doors.

Still. We continue to sit and watch the snowflakes no longer fall and no longer listen while the lights go out.

Still. I watch for you through the window against the night sky before dawn casts shades over the day.

Still. I yet attempt to imagine the moment that encapsulates all moments.

You wait outside the cage watching me pace the room while I watch you stand at the edge of this vast land. Your shadow lengthened but did not fall from me. The dust loosened did not drop from my skin. At her glance I rose and followed her home.

I see you. Through the closed window. I see you. Through the twisted floor boards. I see you. Though you are not there. I see you. You walk by way of distant rooms to this place moving only how you imagine you move. But I see how you move. You stand with your hands cupped around your mouth your lips nearly touching the wall and you whisper. Then you turn your head and press your hands and ear to the wall listening for a reply. Or echo. I watch you do these things. And listen as all you hear is your silence crying back at you.

Inside for long hours we sit watching sallow light from a single window break across the clutter of the room. All is still yet all moves. Together in this corner we watch from where we cannot see the road. Outside a night of iridescent tower blocks stand with their many layered stories howling into the dark.

I whisper to myself as I wander through these anecdote of rooms. The laboured necessity of the ticking clock echoes. This is the place where thoughts morph with performing monkeys and circus horses. I cross with the spider its seven legs holding fast. We sit. Time stirs. I understand now. The boy has left the house and we ought not allow him back. Open all windows and doors so his aura seeps away. We walk to the edge of the incoming sea and hammer flat the waves. After rolling back the skin from the surface of the water we make leaden darts from the sores of each other's bodies and scream at the glare of blood sweeping skyward from our eyes. Unhurried we wander back to the mirage that is our home.

Light radiates from a distant window. Close by on an empty road hangs a lamp under which no one waits. The lamp helps only me along the way away to a house with a single window that looks out at nothing but a nearby light.

At an undefined distance from the city you stand and watch its scheme pour from your tired mind. From the fiction of an empty room you see there is only an empty room. In the dark hours together we watch lights spark from the small sounds generated by the house in its quiet watchfulness. I then systematically turned through the house and lime washed an x on each door before locking it from the inside. Now all is solid. All is real. All is well.

A day awake is the walk across a room. When time inside is equal to time outside thought becomes an impossibility. Isolate the desolate. The dull thud that is a ticking clock is the dumb note of a blunt stake hammered into the back of my head. The room is a stone mask through which I see and breathe and the false face by which I am perceived. Behind the mask the merest scent of a will. A negligible shift in the air. A bleeding stain around an inner wall. What is happening outside. No I hear nothing. I was just wondering. It appears so dark and sounds so quiet. Why is that. How does that feel. What happens when outside is outside.

High towers receive nesting adventurers as here sufficient tales are borne for lesser men to construct a methodology of what later becomes the room of unquestionable inconsequence. Reminiscing leads to confessing. Incalculable undoing. Feel for the right spot break into a sweat and peel another layer of caked rind from the palm of your hand. The storm bobs easily from field to field. Blank tenants condense behind the wash of closed gates. The lessons of agony reap havoc where the tiny dragons indicate the way to Prague Square.

Haemorrhaging circular patterns against cracked skin follows the Newtonian rule for plain paper wrappers each going unseen at the touch of oiled fingers which swell towards the needy black teeth. Pleasure me to walk the concrete grounds as fluorescent screams waft between us and natures' providence jealously listens out. Silver nitrates as totemic beasts pictured through ever widening slats slants a particular sunrise over a completed sentence. Running back to dad's arms is like that. Pack the choices away but hold onto the look. On such days what you are is laid naked to the gaze. On others by habit we use the same word. Redeeming. So influenced I pour out my hours into a drinking cup. A fasting apparition beckons me to break ranks and taste just a morsel from the unusual corners of the bread. I'll kick the can when I am able. A sortie through alleyways finds me alongside a wondering aesthete. Her breath even from there smells sweet. Sit and wait. The gentle heat of fortitude will tailor you respectfully and inoculate you from having to walk burned foot across fractured earth beneath which a giant sleeps.

A fine spring rains. A shower of reflections. A hundred thousand mirrors falling over us. Let's watch ourselves in this small drowning world battle with what we see.

On the trade winds the émigré braces and batters down his isolated chants. Muddy waters are calmed when fine features are caressed against the grain. Pulled back lines speculate on words hatched in the cracks of sun scarce lodgings. Pale nanophiles search for historical inevitability. Today's lesson failed to waken these tired lungs. Outside with backs against the wall the two Manets heard noises. The steps were rewinding quietly behind and an ever drowning spirit rose. A razor lodged in my teeth cut the picture of the trinity from the frame as from the corner of my eye I fitfully watched an occidental panel game. With blank looks for starters the family of spies were beaten by an insomniac grandfather nailed to his room armed only with a box of photographs. Nothing was said. So blow into the wind eat into your past and close tight the door. On each Wednesday write down all that you see creeping in through the wet walls strap finger to finger hold on to your stare and watch as all the day does is brighten the room a little.

She was speaking in a distant room. Her voice unworldly like a forest. Air moved through the house and like a mouth all doors whispered closed. From flitting against the window in the basement they stepped along long corridors each on a path back to a precarious room. The footsteps changed pace on the road outside. Drifting. The movement of her breath faintly echoes as she hovers alone in her room staring into deflected eyes. Light as displacement. Wait by the gate and time will bring you solitude. Outside the enemy tires of their harsh ways. Madonna mocks the misspelled. Crowds march in denouncement of their own shadow.

Lick the sweating walls as a privilege. Ingrain the insulated hands. Tire of awkward falls. Dowse their gleaming eyes. Both keenly look for you. Just as punishment. Let them take what you leave behind. Continue alone. Transportation to a new box. Give. Offer. Imitate. Such tortuous routes and wasted days.

It was yesterday. The text began to rot in my hands. Looking down I watched my fingers empty as the broken words fell in easy drifts to the floor. I wiped the last of the dark dust against the damp window and stared at a most perfect tone of grey sky as it stretched out across the desolate land. It was the morning of a lone night's vigil overlooking the frosty expanse between here and the distant forest that unnoticed I lost all sovereignty over my mind. The Chekhovian cannon in a flurry of asymmetry buries itself deep into burning lungs. The snow capped moon loses an eye. Roads block only those privileged with non-reflectivity. Insensible witnesses attest the veracity of a mirror image. Better now. Feel the warm air reflect from the glass. Touch the wound. The facade that fell in slow-mo onto the distracted crowd made for another troubled day. Avoid the rivulets. Affirm the breed. Face the faceless hoard. Finally affect to shuffle the demons in the out-takes draw but leave well alone.

Now in this place it is cold and the walls are fading. We've been to the centre of the world and now it's time to go. On a hushed night sticking meticulously to the rewritten script she ad-libbed a last telephone call made from the booth standing on a damp street.

In the quiet of a still morning. All passed by.

And so dead were days.

Shorts

Alongside

I saw a mighty cast of trees fall great shadows against a long sweep of hillside. As the sight of this evasive splendour lifted me from the earth so there lay across dry fields the shallow light of a silent crowd revealed as a host of stochastic figurines paused before stepping one by one onto the mirage road. Pills chanced fallen across a floor alongside the petty dress collapsed and scattered inside the bombed house shook as another wall fell. Through a lattice of blue streets the worn foreign feet drift home walking where soft earth dead ends at an inaccessible door. The hum of the pillow against my head accompanies my steps to the edge of town where I stand negative against a vast night. Step over. They bow at the straw wall while picking at messages timed to go off before the last word.

Turn of the Century

A hundred weights tied to a hundred legs of a hundred bodies with a hundred minds sheltering a hundred visions across the hundred lakes swallowing a hundred suicides.

Event horizon

A man standing in a dark room switched on a torch. He traced its light slowly around the walls. When the light hit the uncurtained window it illuminated a man standing outside in the night looking into the room. With both hands this man held a photograph of a face in front of his face like a mask. The photograph was of the face of the man standing in the dark room.

Forming the Past

Swimming in a depthless sea of dreams. Our memories bubble to the surface to form a sky. We might spasmodically look up and see our past through the moving cerulean water. And sometimes float up to momentarily exist where the sky and sea meet.

The Street

A walk in the street is a conversation with all that is held therein.

Synopses

"Your Concrete Arms"
4' 47"

Breathing freedoms defiant observe the quiet thought
as though sitting alone in a room. New suppositions add
to the human trinity. Quondam. Now. And to be. Relief.
Anxiety. Only ghost. As now in the face of ourselves the
dread almighty rule burns up as it falls away back to Earth.
I deduce and abide I. Laughter is mine. As I am I. More
subplots to solipsism. I see a tangible future for that which
is mine. A mechanical star of thought orbiting the eternal
lacuna. That being the void beside me. So I am as I wish. I
am as I touch. I am as I imitate. Rejoice this idle deliberation.
The ideal is past. Now inhabit the lone material. Only as
far as ennoblement. Scepticism scrapes by bleeding at the
knees. Then at the door. Far in the darkness.

"Impasse"
11' 20"

It was if this past had happened to someone else. My memories are another's story told to me. It was the journey to a place I have never been. With a light I have never seen. An air I had never breathed. You were there. Or did I place you. Because I need you to be. A doubtful mind repeatedly struggling with the flow of images. I am sure I was there.

"Without"
4' 48"

In quiet trepidity she waits at the outermost bounds of the world. And looking out through the cracks in death's door she watches in de-saturated light the legion of souls.

"Quiet, This Still Air"
4' 12"

I found my way to a forgotten house.

My journey to this place took me along bleak paths bitter cold from despondent feet and to desolate cities sombre and oppressive racked taut by their grieving. Passing through the stuporous lives of untold people I found comfort in this drifting avidity of souls as I hid in the long shadows of all those irretrievable days.

This place is my home. This place is where complete my past is stored. All the fears and joys of my life rest here. In this place I will revisit my memories for the last time.

"Awake In A Room"
6' 20"

Past illusions increasingly encroach upon the present producing a confused vision of a self and the model of how the world works. Inside and outside are no longer distinguishable. Time shifts in volatile waves. The ever tangible moves beyond reach.

"Between States"
04' 19"

Winter. Evening. Somewhere outside the war zone. Understand the stories of the unknown told by the unseen. Laying plans for an eternity of souls. We wait. Surveying from the shadows.

"Half Light"
08' 23"

Watching the faded Earth pull grain-light from the sky. A voice of elements calls on volatile mortality. In the half light of a misconceived landscape. Each step a protean text. Restless. A crystalline shade.

Breinigsville, PA USA
21 February 2011
256019BV00001B/2/P